The Last-Place Sports Poems of Jeremy Bloom

**A COLLECTION OF POEMS ABOUT WINNING,
LOSING, AND BEING A GOOD SPORT (SOMETIMES)**

The Last-Place Sports Poems of Jeremy Bloom

A COLLECTION OF POEMS ABOUT WINNING, LOSING, AND BEING A GOOD SPORT (SOMETIMES)

Gordon Korman
and
Bernice Korman

SCHOLASTIC INC.
New York Toronto London Auckland Sydney

No part of this publication may be reproduced in whole or in part, or stored in a retrieval system, or transmitted in any form or by any means, electronic, mechanical, photocopying, recording, or otherwise, without written permission of the publisher. For information regarding permission, write to Scholastic Inc., 555 Broadway, New York, NY 10012.

ISBN 0-590-25516-9

12 11   8 9/0

Printed in the U.S.A.   40

First Scholastic printing, October 1996

To the winners, sure, but especially
to the nice guys who finish last.

CONTENTS

INTRODUCTION

The poems in this book are a second chance.

The second chance was offered to Jeremy Bloom by Mrs. Stegowitz, aka Mrs. Stegosaurus.

"Jeremy, I know you're still upset about all those D minuses I gave you last year," she said on registration day at school.

"Oh, that's okay, Mrs. Stegosau — Mrs. Stegowitz," said Jeremy cheerfully. "The D minuses were kind of like my trademark. I was a D-minus poet."

"Well," the teacher admitted, "I might have been a little too hard on you. That's why I'd like you to sign up for my poetry-writing workshop now, in seventh grade."

"But — but you teach novels this year!" Jeremy protested faintly.

"I do," said Mrs. Stegowitz, "but I'm continuing the poetry class because it's so popular. We'd love to have you join us."

"Oh, no thanks," Jeremy replied quickly. He'd already picked out the perfect elective — Media

Studies, popularly called Couch Potato 101. Homework every night was watching TV. Jeremy had been in training for this course all his life. He might have been a D-minus poet, but in staring at the boob tube, he was A + +.

"I've spoken to the Principal," coaxed Mrs. Stegowitz. "She said that if you can pull your grade up this year, we can also raise last year's D minus. What do you say?"

Jeremy didn't answer. He was watching in horror as a COURSE FULL sticker was placed over the sign advertising Couch Potato 101. Oh, no! The noose was tightening around his neck. He pictured himself back writing poems for Mrs. Stegosaurus. There had to be some way out!

"Well, uh — last year kind of burned me out on ideas, so I wouldn't know what to write about —"

"Any subject," beamed the teacher. "Whatever gets your creative juices flowing. What are your interests?"

"None!" Jeremy blurted, breaking into a cold sweat. "No interests! I'm a really boring guy!"

At that very moment, Jeremy's two best friends, Michael and Chad, burst onto the scene.

"We did it!" crowed Michael. "We just signed up for football, soccer, hockey, basketball, and baseball!"

"For all three of us!" added Chad excitedly. "This is going to be our best year yet!"

"There, you see?" exclaimed Mrs. Stegowitz triumphantly. "That's what you're going to write about — sports!"

"But — but —"

That was all Jeremy got to say in his own defense. Before he knew it, his name was on the class list.

Jeremy Bloom was a poet again.

PART

I

FOOTBALL SEASON

September 5 to October 31

I

FOOTBALL SEASON

The first poems of Jeremy Bloom's second poetic career were written while he was the backup tight end for the York Middle School seventh-grade football team, the Yeomen.

Michael and Chad had also made the team, and the three were ecstatic to be Yeomen. In celebration of the team name, they were constantly yelling *"Yo, man!"* followed by wild laughter and high fives. For this reason, many of the football season poems were written after school in the detention room.

With a consistent passing game, and a tough defense, the Yeomen were the team to beat in the county. Jeremy was overjoyed. He lived, breathed, and ate football — and wrote about it.

OUR NUMBER ONE FAN

We had a decent season,
　　We won nine, lost only six.
I really liked my teammates,
　　And picked up a few new tricks.

We get together now and then
　　To talk of fun we had.
But if you think that we were psyched,
　　You should have seen my dad!

He didn't sit all season long,
　　He cheered, his face bright pink.
He cheered when we were playing well,
　　Cheered louder when we'd stink.

And when we went on offense,
　　He would really lose control.
He treated every handoff
　　Like it was the Super Bowl.

He smeared blue makeup on his face
　　To match our uniforms.
And rooted on through bitter cold,
　　And violent thunderstorms.

He went ballistic once or twice,
    Got thrown out of the stands.
But afterwards he'd find us,
    Trays of hot dogs in his hands.

And Cokes for all the guys to drink,
    While he said something kind
About the refs — "it's not *their* fault
    That they're completely blind."

And who threw us the party
    At the season's end? My dad!
But I can sense that since that day
    The guy's been kind of sad.

Now, hockey starts this weekend;
    And to make the team would thrill him.
But I just hope that all of the
    Excitement doesn't kill him!

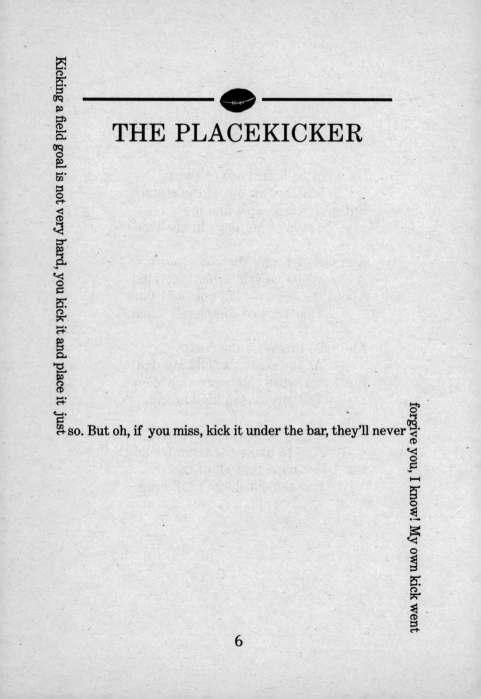

THE PLACEKICKER

Kicking a field goal is not very hard, you kick it and place it just so. But oh, if you miss, kick it under the bar, they'll never forgive you, I know! My own kick went wild, missed the uprights completely, was miles away when it came down. And we lost the game and the championship too! Now I can't show my face in this town!

INJURIES

Our quarterback just broke his leg.
The instant he went down,
He automatically became
The hero of our town.

Well, since I'm on the Ping-Pong team,
I really must complain,
'Cause no one ever gave a hoot
About my pinkie sprain.

THE SUPER BOWL

The Super Bowl — it's Super-great!
But watch that you don't suffocate
In Super-hoopla, Super-hype,
As broadcasters spew Super-tripe

Of Super-teams we're here to see
Play Super-offense, Super-D,
And dish out Super-hits and hurts,
While Super-stores sell Super-shirts,

And Super-hot dogs, Super-drinks,
Who cares if the *game* always stinks?
They come in airplanes, cars, and trucks,
Those Super-seats cost Super-bucks!

Not counting souvenirs you trash
Upon returning from this bash.
A Super-costly Super-trip —
Your Super-team lost forty-zip!

September 28

The Yeomen were 3 and 0, and tied for first place, when Mrs. Stegowitz announced that she would be at the game on Saturday.

"I want to see you in action," the teacher explained to Jeremy. "That way I'll have a better understanding of the motivation behind your poetry."

It was a spectacular fall day, crisp and sunny, and York Middle School was up 14–7 in the third quarter. But Mrs. Stegowitz still hadn't arrived. Jeremy was in for the regular tight end, and the Yeomen were marching down the field, first down after first down.

"Hike!"

Jeremy bounced off the line and felt a perfect pass smack into his chest. He closed his arms on the ball and started for the goal line — past the 40, the 35, the 30 . . .

"Yoo-hoo, Jeremy!"

Out of the corner of his eye, Jeremy spotted a figure in a bright red coat standing up in the bleachers. It was Mrs. Stegowitz, waving and cheering.

CRUNCH!

The opposing safety came out of nowhere and rammed into Jeremy at full speed. Stunned, Jeremy went flying. So did the ball. There was a huge bruising pileup as both teams dove for the fumble. But the football bounced through a dozen grasping hands and rolled right back to Jeremy.

Woozy, he grabbed it, struggled upright, and headed downfield. He could feel the vibration of running feet pounding along the turf behind him. A voice — Chad's, he thought — was screaming encouragement. What was he saying?

"Stop, you idiot! You're going the wrong way!"

Wrong way?! Jeremy pulled up short on the one-yard line. Michael and Chad plowed into him like a freight train.

The ball squirted loose and went blooping into the end zone. It was pounced on by an opposing player. Touchdown.

It was only 7 points, but the Yeomen never seemed to get back on track after such a humiliating disaster. Perhaps Michael put it best when he said, "They should have called us the *Woe*-men!"

Easy passes were dropped, tackles missed; kicks went wild. The team lost the game, and every other one they played after that, finishing out the season in last place.

Suddenly, Jeremy Bloom couldn't bear to think about football, so writing about it was out of the question. The word "football" scarcely appeared again in his poems.

THE SPECTATOR

I showed the coach my fielding style;
He told me with a crooked smile:
  "Some of us play, and some of us watch.
  Perhaps you just don't have good hands.
  Some of us play, and some of us watch,
  And your place is there in the stands."

I showed the coach the way I dribble;
He didn't even try to quibble:
  "Some of us play, and some of us watch;
  All talents cannot be the same.
  Some of us play, and some of us watch.
  Now, sit down and take in the game."

I showed the coach my soccer skill;
He heaved a sigh, and took a pill:
  "Some of us play, and some of us watch,
  And though I don't want to sound curt,
  Some of us play and some of us watch.
  Sit down, kid, before you get hurt."

I showed the coach the way I skate;
He didn't even hesitate:
  "Some of us play, and some of us watch;
  Some athletes are not meant to be.
  Some of us play and some of us watch.
  You look like a watcher to me."

EXCUSES

It's best to have the running back,
The smooth athletic skater,
The Golden Glove, the MVP,
Well, nothing could be greater!

The point guard with quick magic hands
Is sure to have his uses.
But who's the guy worth solid gold?
The one with the excuses!

Football: The gridiron was crooked!
The goalposts weren't straight!
But otherwise my kick
was perfectly great!

Baseball: My reason for failure
I cannot disguise.
I missed because sunshine
was right in my eyes!

Hockey: It's not fair! My playing
has always been steady!
I was sick! I was absent!
I just wasn't ready!

Fishing: The hook was defective!
The lake was too deep!
The con-man who sold me
these worms was a creep!

Tennis: The umpire refused me
the breaks I deserve!
That tall guy was using
an illegal serve!

Figure Skating: My skate lace was broken!
My coach wasn't there!
The judges were cheating!
It just wasn't fair!

So load your team with superstars.
It's really not the same
As having that one guy who's good
At passing off the blame.

PART

II

---⚽---

SOCCER SEASON

November 1 to December 22

II

SOCCER SEASON

The second phase of Jeremy Bloom's sports poems was written while he was a member of the My-Choice Puppy Chow Falcons soccer team.

Once again, Jeremy, Michael, and Chad were teamed up, composing cheers to "the old purple and gold," and practicing by bouncing anything lighter than a bowling ball off their heads. Consequently, many of the soccer season poems were written in the nurse's office.

In no time at all, every other word out of Jeremy's mouth was "soccer," and the Bloom house was in the grip of My-Choice mania. So were Jeremy's poems.

NO HEADS

I suppose I like soccer.
It's really quite fun.
The field is gigantic,
You kick and you run.

You don't use your hands,
It's all footwork instead,
But the ball can be bounced
Off the top of your head,

Which gives you a headache.
It's also hard work,
And — this is the worst part —
You look like a jerk.

You run down the field
For the ball, win the race,
And pass it along
With a smash of your face.

So if anyone wants me
To play this dumb game,
They really should change
All the parts that are lame.

I don't mind the field,
Which is fifty miles long,
I don't even mind
The team's silly fight song.

I don't mind the goal,
Which is ninety feet wide,
And deep enough for
A whole army to hide.

And I really don't mind
Those dumb shorts we all wear,
Or the running around,
First to here, then to there.

But being a doofus
Is something I dread,
So I'm *not* going to bounce
The ball off of my head!

THE ATHLETE'S PRAYER

Today
Is our big game,
The one to decide who's the best team in town,
    And who gets the trophy,
        And the glory,
            And who eats dirt.

If we lose
(Which is a distinct possibility)
When the ball goes into our net,
Please, please, please
    Don't let it
        Bounce off my knee,
            my nose,
            my elbow,
            my chest,
            my earlobe,
            my eyebrow,
    and especially not my derriere
                        First!

TRANSFORMATION

My soccer coach was really mad,
Which made the players very sad,
Oh, what a rotten game we had!
We're bad.

Our uniforms are shocking pink,
Our captain is a little dink,
No wonder all the players think
We stink.

We went into an eight-game slide,
And our despair was bona fide,
We practiced extra on the side —
We tried.

We found the dink could really run!
We started having lots of fun;
One Sunday when the game was done —
We won!

From now on, every soccer mate
Has confidence in how we rate,
And we have cause to celebrate —
We're great!

November 22

When Mrs. Stegowitz decided to attend a soccer game, Jeremy made sure to put her in the front row.

"Best seats in the house," he promised her. "You'll see everything."

But what he really meant was that *he* would see *her*. That way she couldn't startle him like at the football game. She wasn't wearing her red coat this time, but she would still be easy to keep an eye on because of her hat. It was a puffy round white cap, decorated with large black dots.

Their opponents were one of the best teams in the league, but the Falcons were holding their own in a hard-fought battle. The score was tied at 2, and My-Choice Puppy Chow was going all out to break the deadlock. The play swung by in front of the bleachers where the spectators sat cheering. All ten Falcon forwards charged after the ball, and the crowd rose to its feet in excitement.

A gust of wind picked Mrs. Stegowitz's hat up off her head. It sailed out onto the field, and came down in the thick of the play. And suddenly there were *two* round white objects with black spots out there on the field.

As a unit, the Falcons fell on the hat, kicking

madly, trying to pass it to each other. By the time they realized it wasn't the ball, their opponents were thundering down the field in a ten-man breakaway. As they celebrated the go-ahead goal, they were laughing and pointing at the humiliated Falcons, who were still kicking at the battered, mud-caked hat.

The wheels came off of Jeremy's soccer team. As Michael put it, "My-Choice Puppy Chow was dog meat!"

This debacle cost them the game, which triggered a losing streak that stretched till the end of the season. At one point, they went six games without even scoring a goal — setting a league record as they landed themselves in last place.

Soccer went from Jeremy's favorite sport to his worst nightmare — and vanished completely from his poems.

CHESS

Who says that chess is not a sport?
Athletics for the brain!
And if you think it isn't hard,
Allow me to explain.

Now, any jerk can throw a ball;
Baboons can learn to skate;
But playing chess is something else —
You have to concentrate.

The strategies are quite complex,
And that's my favorite part.
You really can't be good at chess
Unless you're very smart.

And bold and strong, aggressive too;
You cannot hesitate
In this, the military game
Of capture, check, and mate.

I know I'm not a master yet,
I'm sure I will improve
As soon as I can work out how
Those funny pieces move.

⚽

INJURY REPORT HAIKU

Pulled groin, broken foot
Heel spur, charley horse, and bruised
Sa-cro-il-i-ac.

GONE COMMERCIAL

I'm gonna be a superstar;
    of that I have no doubt,
But I will not be known for all
    the batters I strike out,
Or power plays, or touchdowns, or
    my brutal slam-dunk force,
My super-fame will come from all
    the products I endorse.

From underwear, to limousines,
    to matzo balls by Herschel,
I'll be the guy to catch your eye,
    the star of each commercial.
My famous face will do the job
    far more than words could tell.
They won't say, "Man, can that guy play!"
    they'll say, "Man, can he sell!"

On billboards pushing toothpaste,
    and on every tuna tin,
No oatmeal box is printed
    without my infectious grin.
My voice is on the radio,
    my face is on TV —
You wouldn't buy a paper clip
    unless it came from me!

So though I'm not that good at sports,
I'll make it just the same.
Some day my face will hang in the
Endorsement Hall of Fame.

PART
III

HOCKEY SEASON

January 3 to March 10

III

HOCKEY SEASON

Hockey season was the backdrop for the next batch of Jeremy's poems.

He and Chad and Michael all skated for Pretty Polly Wallpaper. They were the Jets, which didn't seem to have too much to do with wallpaper. But that didn't stop the three from squawking "Polly want a cracker!" night and day, and even in class. They also practiced skating in their stocking feet along the polished corridors of the school. This caused countless collisions and pileups, and even one spectacular tumble down the school's back stairs. For this reason, many of the hockey season poems were written in the bathtub while the poet soaked away bruises, aches, and pains.

Pretty Polly played a grueling style of hard-checking hockey, and Jeremy walked taller and squared his shoulders at all times, even while sleeping. No subject besides hockey ever captured his attention. This was especially evident in his poems.

THE WINGER RINGER

Billy is a checker,
Bobby is a wrecker,
Talbot's in the play in every scene;
But if I were choosing guys
For talent, smarts, and size,
I'd always draft a girl named Josephine.

Josephine's a friend
Who'll back you to the end,
And break her neck to help support the team;
She's also pretty tough,
And likes her hockey rough,
A winger who is held in high esteem.

Thomas is a skater,
Fred a goal creator,
Albert is a guy who comes to play;
Jonathan is lean,
And Jay is extra mean,
But Josephine can blow them all away.

MY TRADEMARK MOVE

Orr had his spin-o-rama,
Gretzky, his behind-the-net wraparound.
All marquee hockey players
Perfect a trademark move.

Mine is skating full speed
Into the boards, stick first
Jamming the butt-end
Deep into my stomach.

It won't help me make the NHL,
But it will give me
A unique perspective
On how a shish kebab must feel.

ZAMBONI

I'm not a real big hockey fan,
I think it's kind of phoney.
It would be better if they played
Along with the Zamboni.

Just think of the tremendous boost
That it would give a team,
To have that big Zamboni
Bearing down the ice full steam.

It really seems insane to me
For every game to start
With someone driving off the ice
The most exciting part!

Those pampered, stuck-up superstars
Who think that they're in clover,
Will make their fancy moves while
Trying not to get run over.

And all the big defensemen,
So rough and tough and mean,
Let's see them try to bodycheck
A seven-ton machine.

They'll play Zamboni bumper cars,
The action will be hot;
We'll see the evolution of
The new Zamboni-shot.

The NHL will honor me.
They'll see that it's baloney
To try to play a hockey game
Excluding the Zamboni!

CELEBRATION

You've won a major contest.
The moment's super-bright!
And yet it doesn't count unless
You celebrate it right.

Leap in the air!
Rip at your hair!
Dance with great flair!

Go on a spree!
Fling some debris!
Howl with such glee!

Rile up the crowd!
Leave the rest cowed!
Bellowing loud!

It's a dream!
What a team!
S - C - R - E - A - M !!!

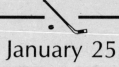

January 25

When Mrs. Stegowitz expressed interest in taking in a hockey game, Michael and Chad were skeptical.

"Mrs. Stegosaurus doesn't have another hat, does she?" Chad asked. "And maybe this one looks like a puck?" Chad was a pretty sarcastic guy sometimes.

"Don't be stupid!" Jeremy scoffed. "It's indoors, so she won't wear a hat. Plus I'll get her to sit in the back. Nothing can go wrong. I guarantee it."

Sure enough, at game time, Mrs. Stegowitz was in the very last row of seats, right up against the arena scoreboard.

The game was end-to-end action. The Pretty Polly Jets were the superior team, but the opposing goalie was making some spectacular saves. His brilliant play was preserving a narrow 2–1 lead over the Jets.

Suddenly, a lead pass found Jeremy in the clear. He spun around and charged for the net on a clean breakaway, intent on tying the score at 2. He crossed the red line! He crossed the blue line!

The spectators roared to their feet, and with them rose Mrs. Stegowitz. As she flung her arms over her head, her purse swung back into the scoreboard, hitting the button that reset the game clock. The timer immediately went to zero, and the green light came on. The siren howled, signifying the end of the period.

Deflated and disappointed, Jeremy stopped in his tracks.

"Keep playing!" bellowed the referee. *"The period's not over yet!"*

WHAM!

A defenseman blindsided Jeremy. His helmet went one way, his stick another, but Jeremy himself was propelled straight through the goalie's legs into the net. The puck, unfortunately, wasn't with him.

According to Michael, "That was when Pretty Polly Wallpaper came unglued." The Jets gave up five unanswered goals, to lose 7–1. And that was only the beginning of a long slide. Playing like stumblebums on ice, the Jets earned sole possession of last place.

Jeremy tore down all his hockey posters and stopped nagging his parents for a trip to the Hockey Hall of Fame. And write poems about this rotten sport? Not in a million years!

MONOPOLY

"Take a walk on the Boardwalk,"
Who owns it? Is it me?
   It's mine, with one big red hotel,
   Two thousand dollars' fee!

But I got there by doubles,
So I don't have to pay.

     Do so!
Do not!
     Do so!
Do not!
'Cause that's the way we play!

Okay, but that's my railroad,
The good old B & O.
   I'll pay you when I've got the bucks;
   I'll soon be passing GO.

What am I? Chase Manhattan Bank?
You have to pay right now!

     Says who?
Says me!
     Oh, yeah?
That's right!
     Okay, don't have a cow.

. . . four . . . five . . . six — Free Parking!
I rake in all that cash!
No way. That isn't in the rules!
That's one big load of trash!

But everybody plays that way!
You mean just crooks like you?

Am not!
Are so!
Am not!
Are so!
I get it all! It's true!

You've landed on the Water Works.
I've got three houses there.
You can't build on utilities!
You're cheating! It's not fair!

Big talk from someone who's so dumb
He thought he could buy Jail.

No way!
Yes, way!
Shut up!
You're nuts!
Well, you approved the sale!

41

I've raised the rent on my St. James.
We must be playing different games!
I saw that! You just stole Park Place!
I oughta smash you in the face!

Just try!
      Hold still!
Go home!
      I will!
          Push —
          Pull —
          Gasp —
          Snort —
Monopoly's a grueling sport.

THE WANDERER

I'm suffering from wanderlust,
I've got the travel bug,
So I must hit the highway
To follow nature's tug.

The need to see the wide wide world
Is prickling at my scalp.
I have to head for Europe
And climb myself an Alp,

To tramp through broadleaf forests,
And breathe the morning haze.
With oceans to discover,
And brand-new trails to blaze!

To march the plains, sail rivers,
To see what I can see —
I leave first thing tomorrow;
Tonight there's great TV.

PART
IV

BASKETBALL SEASON

March 12 to April 25

IV

BASKETBALL SEASON

While he was point guard for the Joe's Septic Tank Company Knicks, Jeremy continued to write poems throughout basketball season.

Jeremy was a terrific ball handler with a great jump shot, although his rebounding was a little weak. For this reason, many of the poems of the basketball season were composed mentally while he hung from the jungle gym, trying to get taller.

Everybody said the Knicks had chemistry. And while Jeremy didn't have the faintest idea what this meant, that didn't stop him from bragging about it to anyone who would listen. Even the refrigerator repairman had to hear about the mighty Knicks. So it was hardly surprising that Jeremy's poetry developed a basketball feel.

S - T - R - E - T - C - H

Basketball is everything!
It's always been my dream
To deke and sky and dunk and fly,
And play for my school team.

But there's an awful problem
No one can seem to fix:
The team height starts at six foot four,
And I am four foot six.

I'm sure to grow, the coach says;
I'll shoot right up, and then
I'll deke and sky and dunk and fly.
The question here is — when?

It might take till I'm thirty,
That's what I greatly fear,
For I'll no longer be in school —
(Miss Mott says I'll be here.)

I've got to do some growing
(Is there a stretching pill?),
I won't be here at thirty!
(Miss Mott says yes, I will.)

I shall not be discouraged,
I'll never shut the door.
Someday when I sit on the bench
My feet will reach the floor!

I'll make it to the court, then,
To play for my school team.
I'll deke and sky and dunk and fly —
It's always been my dream.

ODE TO THE NERF BASKETBALL HOOP OVER MY DESK

Bloom . . . for three . . . it's good!
Nothing but net!
Here's Bloom . . . driving the lane . . .
He elevates over the defense . . .
What a monster dunk! . . . the backboard shatters!

Bloom again . . . time's running out . . .
4 . . . 3 . . . 2 . . .
He throws up a desperation shot . . .
Swish! Unbelievable! Bloom has won the champion-
    ship . . .
The crowd rushes the court . . .

"Why isn't your homework ready, young man?"

LOCAL HERO

The local paper says I'm great;
I fear I must agree.
Of all the players on the team,
There's no one good as me.

I dribble like a wizard, and
My jump shot is pure art.
The way I crash the boards is like
Raw talent a la carte.

My passing is so delicate,
The coaches swoon and sigh.
In all this town no player is
As masterful as I.

I point with pride to all this praise,
And I puff out my chest.
Of all my qualities, they like
My modesty the best.

MERCURY

I want to go to the planet Mercury.

Not for the scenery,
Because half the planet is always dark,
So you couldn't see it anyway.

Not for the climate,
Which is 400 degrees in winter,
And would fry you like an egg.

Not for the people,
Because nobody lives there,
And can you really blame them?

But I want to go to Mercury
For the gravity,
Which is one fifth that of Earth.

And even though I'm four foot two,
And can't jump,
And everybody calls me Lump-man,

On Mercury, I could dunk a basketball.

March 26

The Knicks just seemed to click. They had four wins with only one loss when Mrs. Stegowitz mentioned a sudden interest in basketball. Michael and Chad were horrified.

"No way, Bloom!" growled Chad. "That woman is a jinx!"

"She's death!" Michael agreed. "Tell her she can't come — or *you* can't come!"

"What a couple of dopes!" Jeremy sneered. "It was easy to get rid of Mrs. Stegosaurus. I told her tip-off was at five o'clock. The game starts at three. We'll be done by four-thirty the latest!"

Sure enough, when they arrived at the YMCA gym, there was no sign of Mrs. Stegowitz. Just as they were exchanging high fives of congratulations, the news arrived by phone: The referee had a flat tire on the freeway, and there would be a short delay.

By 4:45, Jeremy was bathed in sweat. Cautiously, he opened the dressing room door and poked his head out.

"Yoo-hoo — Jeremy!" Mrs. Stegowitz waved and beckoned.

Irrationally, Jeremy panicked. He bolted down

the corridor, his teacher hot on his heels.

"Jeremy — it's me! Mrs. Stegowitz!"

Jeremy ran harder, twisting and turning through the labyrinth of halls in the YMCA basement. Soon he had lost Mrs. Stegowitz, but he was lost too. He wandered for a few agonizing minutes before reaching the court just as the referee came rushing in.

The beginning of the game was pure torture for Jeremy. Just knowing that Mrs. Stegowitz was out there, and could appear at any moment, spooked him. But by the second half, he assumed that she had blundered back to the parking lot and gone home. Surely nobody could be lost in the YMCA for all this time!

He began to relax and concentrate on the game, a tough contest that went right down to the wire. With eight seconds left and the Knicks trailing by a point, Chad passed him the ball just inside the foul line. Jeremy took aim for the easy game-winning jump shot.

Just as he was about to release the ball, there was a whirring of machinery, and the basket began to rise. Before his astonished eyes, it lifted straight up, then tilted back, away from the court. At the same time, the mechanical curtain of the gym's stage parted to reveal Mrs. Stegowitz, her finger still on the control button.

"Oh, *there* you are!" she called. "Who's winning?"

The game-ending buzzer answered that question. The Knicks had lost by a point.

"Well," was Michael's philosophical comment, "I guess that was when Joe's Septic Tank Company started to go down the toilet."

The Knicks never recovered from the case of the disappearing basket. Who could shoot while half-expecting the target to float up, up, and away? Scoring, rebounds, steals, and blocked shots dropped to the bottom of the statistics sheet, and so did the Knicks — last place.

Basketball became a dirty word to Jeremy, and he certainly wasn't going to use profanity in his poems.

LUNCHROOM ATHLETICS

Benjamin Beckworth, the calculus whiz,
Is constantly showing how clever he is,
Not only at math, but geography too.
At history and French he's lots better than you.
His science fair projects — they win every year!
There's *nobody* smarter, or — not around here!
He even likes Shakespeare! So help me! No lie!
Which proves there is something not right with this guy.

He'd rather be reading than hanging around,
That's why, at exam time, he's top of the mound.
But in spite of all that, he's a pretty nice guy,
A friend who supports you, and never asks why.
So I'm always forgiving him, time after time,
'Cause having a brain isn't really a crime.
Yet, I have to admit in the lunchroom today,
When *I* won the milk-snorting contest that way,
The milk only dripped out of Benjamin's nose,
While mine was a torrent, like out of a hose!
I felt a great joy, and a great triumph too,
'Cause I can do something the genius can't do!

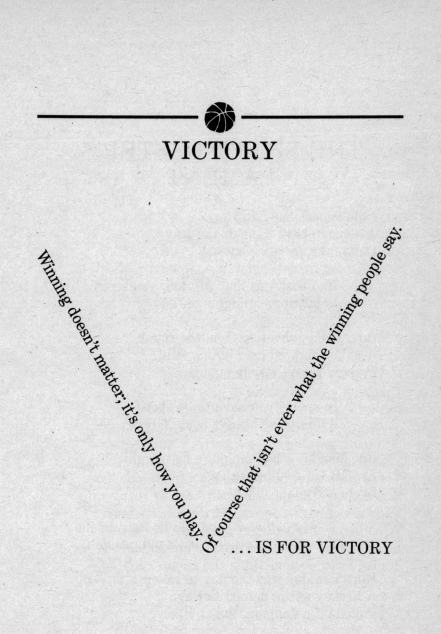

VICTORY

Winning doesn't matter, it's only how you play.

Of course that isn't ever what the winning people say.

. . . IS FOR VICTORY

THE SPORTSCASTER'S LAMENT

I did report one Saturday
A shortstop by the name of Kay
Dove for a *terrific* play.

      And that was fine. My job, you see,
      Is putting highlights on TV.

On Sunday, shooting from the rough,
A golfer showed *astounding* stuff.
Terrific wasn't strong enough.

      In sports you have to be specific.
      Astounding always beats *terrific*.

But Monday made me quite distraught.
An NBA guard hit a shot
From sixty feet, likely as not.

      To say *astounding* would be horrendous.
      This play was more. It was *stupendous*.

Now Tuesday was the day to rave.
A hockey goalie named LeFave
Pulled off a flopping, full-split save.

The word *stupendous* was a fossil
To call a play so darned *colossal*.

On Wednesday, though quite accidental,
A tennis shot was *monumental*.
A track meet got near *transcendental*.

A Thursday fight was *unbelievable*.
But Friday topped that — *inconceivable*.

I know it's wrong to sulk and pout,
But with so many plays to tout,
My adjectives have just run out!

PART

V

BASEBALL SEASON

April 26 to June 16

V

BASEBALL SEASON

Baseball season heralded the coming of spring.

Once again, Jeremy was playing for his school as shortstop for the York Middle School Astros. With Chad at first base and Michael at second, they spent countless hours training to be the deadliest double-play combination in seventh-grade athletics. For this reason, many of the baseball season poems were brainstormed while the poet lay in the bushes, hiding from irate neighbors with broken windows.

The Astros started off with five straight wins. In his mind, Jeremy was buying lumber for a trophy case. In his poems, the solar system was a huge ballpark, with planet-sized baseballs orbiting a giant home plate against an outfield of stars.

THE DREAM SEASON

Our baseball team was 0 and 12,
We never scored a run,
The coach was mean and crabby, and
We didn't have much fun.

It rained for every game we played,
And warped most of our bats,
But we were envy of the league —
We had the coolest hats.

SUPPORT YOUR
LOCAL PITCHER

Attaway, Freddie!
No batter up there!
Pitch him in close!
Brush him back, part his hair!
Whack! It's a homer!
Oh, man, watch it go!
Who told our manager
Freddie could throw?

21ST-CENTURY BASEBALL

Baseball is a boring sport
The way it's always played.
But what if we replace the ball
With, say, a hand grenade?

There'd be no lollygagging then,
The game would not be slow.
A routine fly is not routine
Because the ball might blow.

The new revolving pitcher's mound
Would help speed up the pace.
The pitcher doesn't throw in time?
The ball goes to third base!

The bull pen houses angry bulls,
The warning track is mined,
The umpires are all ninjas,
So you shouldn't call them blind.

There are some special batting pants,
They're lined with firecrackers.
That superstar should really earn
His seven million smackers!

Oh, we'll still call it baseball.
I wouldn't change the name.
But with these small adjustments
It's a more exciting game.

A VIEW FROM THE MOUND

Two cunning pitches are all that I've got.
One is a fastball; the other is not.

My first is like lightning; the speed is intense;
My second the batter pokes over the fence.

But I do not fear this, for he'll never know
Which one of my pitches I'm planning to throw.

TIME TO QUIT

When the coach's wife makes liver
for the team's preseason bash,
and you're the only one to show up
in a tie,

And the shortstop's brother hates you
for no reason, and he's massive,
with a tattoo that says CRUSHER
on his thigh,

When your uniforms
are ugly polyester,
and the night before your first game
you're developing a zit,

And your father's Buick
breaks down on the freeway
while you're en route to the ballpark,
then you know it's time to quit!

When you take your lead off second,
and your jockstrap needs adjusting,
and they tag you
with your hand inside your belt,

And the coach gives you a lecture
from a distance of an inch

and he had onions
on his lunchtime tuna-melt,

When the other team erupts in celebration
when you come up to the plate
because they know
you'll never hit,

And the dugout smells like mothballs, and the
shortstop's brother taunts you from the bleachers,
then you're sure
it's time to quit!

BUT . . .

When you're down eleven–nothing
in the bottom of the second,
and the thunderstorm you pray for does arrive,

And the shortstop's brother has to go to Utah,
and you're thinking that you just might make it
through this year alive,

When you hit the winning homer
in a game in extra innings,
you're a hero, and you really must admit

That in baseball there is no such thing
as lying down and dying —
you're a *player* and it's never time to quit!

May 10

When Mrs. Stegowitz announced that she was a monster baseball fan, Jeremy was ready. He had prepared an elaborate lie about a dentist appointment in Antarctica. But when the time came, all he could manage was, "Oh, please, please, don't come! You're killing us! Have a heart and stay home!"

"Was she upset?" asked Michael at batting practice before the game.

"Nah, she was pretty cool," replied Jeremy. "She promised to stay away. Her husband is the traffic reporter for WGRK, and she's going to work with him for the day. We're in the clear."

Jeremy, Michael, and Chad all had hits, playing a big part in the offense as the Astros opened up a three-run lead. But things got hairy in the fourth inning when the visiting team loaded the bases with only one out.

Jeremy frowned. "Does anybody hear a noise?"

Before anyone could answer, the batter hit a sharp grounder to Jeremy at shortstop. It was what they had been practicing for from the start — the perfect double-play ball! Heart racing, Jeremy scooped it up.

The distant sound swelled to a roar, and an enormous wind swirled around the field, kicking up a huge cloud of dust. As Jeremy looked to throw to second, he saw not Michael but a small bubble helicopter with WGRK TRAFFICOPTER printed on the Plexiglas. The chopper thumped to a jerky landing, and out ran a man and a woman.

Jeremy gawked. "Mrs. Stegosaurus! You *promised*!"

"It was an emergency landing!" the teacher quavered. "We were out of fuel!"

Through the settling dust, Jeremy watched the go-ahead run cross the plate. Eight runs later, York Middle School suffered their first loss.

In Michael's words, "The Astros went supernova, and got fried!"

To have its jinx descend from the heavens directly onto the infield would be enough to send any team into a tailspin. The Astros only held one lead for the rest of the season, and that was erased by a rainout. The final standings told the sad story — once again, last place.

Jeremy was so disgusted with baseball that he couldn't even stomach a Baby Ruth candy bar. And his poems moved as far out of the ballpark as the monster home runs hit by the Astros' opponents.

A SUPERIOR GAME

I must report . . .
>   Hockey's too violent,
>   And baseball is slow,
>   Basketball's silly,
>   As you all must know,
>   Soccer's too simple,
>   A real piece of cake,
>   Golf is so boring,
>   You can't stay awake,

That's why I follow . . .

Venezuelan Indoor Division 3 Blindfolded Pogo Stick Flamethrower Archery . . .

>   Now, that's a sport!

THE EASIEST THING

There's just nothing to it, they told me,
It's the easiest thing ever done,
You open the gate,
                    and put out one skate,
And prepare to have acres of fun.
So I did it, 'cause I'm a believer.
As I sat there and tightened each lace,
I could see myself gliding and spinning —
But instead I fell flat on my face!

It's basic to baseball, they told me,
It's the easiest thing ever done,
You give a great swing
                    with that hickory thing —
The result has to be a home run!
So I did it, with full concentration,
And I managed no homer. Instead,
The ball went straight up, out of sight in the sky,
And came down on the top of my head!

It's very straightforward, they told me,
It's the easiest thing that's around.
For tackles so neat,
                    you just leave your feet
And take the guy down to the ground.
Well, I did it, so brave and ferocious,
Pushing off with a thrust from the toes,
And achieved such a great three-point landing —
My two knees and the tip of my nose!

Basketball's simple, they told me,
It's the easiest thing you can do,
You deke and you fly
                    past that six foot eight guy,
The one with the size nineteen shoe.
So I did it; I'm not sure what happened,
But I know it's pure luck I'm not dead!
That tall guy had hands twice the size of his feet,
And I think that he slam-dunked my head!

Golf is just great, they all told me.
It's the easiest game of them all —
Fresh air, a long walk,
               concentration — no talk,
And you follow this little white ball.
So I tried it, and now I've been out here
One night and two terrible days.
Won't somebody send paramedics?
'Cause I can't find my way in this maze!

Giving up sports, they all told me —
It's the easiest thing that can be.
You put down your bat,
               and equipment like that,
And you watch all those games on TV.
So I did it, and I'd like to tell you
That it's good for knees, shoulders, and hips.
You just need a couch, and a widescreen TV,
And a wheelbarrow loaded with chips.

PART
VI

LAST-RESORT SPORTS

June 26 to August 19

VI

LAST-RESORT SPORTS

Jeremy, Michael, and Chad devoted their summer to trying their hands at every sport known to man. As Jeremy put it, "I will not rest until I find something to *not* stink at!"

The three boys hacked up a golf course, risked their lives on Rollerblades, cycled through torrential rain, and roasted on the tennis court in 90-degree heat. Jeremy nearly beheaded Chad with a boomerang. Michael came close to putting a fencing foil through his own foot. All three found out how many concrete blocks a karate novice can break with his hand — none. And how pole-vaulting looks like much more fun than it is — also none. No fun at all. Even less than that.

Still, the intrepid last-place athletes forged on.

And Jeremy continued to write poems about the sports they played and the ones they only dreamed of.

"You're nuts, man!" Michael accused. "Why would anybody want to write poems in the *summer*?"

"How do you think I deal with all our disasters?" Jeremy replied. "My writing gets me through the bad times."

"*All* our times are 'the bad times,'" mourned Chad, rubbing the boomerang bruise on his neck.

"But it's stupid," Michael persisted. "I mean, you're not in a poetry class anymore. Nobody's ever going to read your poems."

"Oh, I'm sending them all to Mrs. Stegosaurus," Jeremy said with a grin. "She owes me that much. And it's foolproof. How can she zap me through the mail?"

POOL OF DREAMS

Of all water polo teams
Who have swum this pool of dreams
There's the legend of the guy they call "The Bones."
Oh, the tales they tell of him —
How he couldn't even swim!
But he played the game, courageous Harry Jones.

How the little guy did blunder!
You could see his head go under!
He was skinny — we politely called him "slim,"
Through the game we watched him sinking;
Half the pool the kid was drinking!
But the winning goal? For sure it came from him!

Oh, we had a celebration
That awoke our quiet nation,
And we sang aloud in ultra-joyful tones,
But our hero didn't party,
Wasn't hale and loud and hearty,
Why, we couldn't find our winner, good old Bones!

And we never *ever* found him,
But we're sure the water drowned him.
Oh, we searched, but not a smidgen did remain.
So we all got choked and teary,
And our captain had this theory
That they pulled the plug and Bones went down the
    drain.

ORIENTEERING

If you can read a compass well
And map out all the ground,
Then you are sure of knowing how
To find your way around.

And so I signed up gladly
For the course with Mr. Black,
Who'd take us out and lose us,
And we'd make our own way back.

We listened to the lessons,
And we practiced with good cheer,
And now we're in the wilderness.
Oh, where the heck is here?

I'm sure the path is one big loop!
I've passed that rock before!
Please come and get me, Mr. Black,
I can't *stand* any more!

If I get out of this big mess,
I never more will roam.
The compass says which way is north,
But not which way is home.

FIGURE SKATING

Double axel,
Triple jump.

Pirouetting,
And . . . ka-whump!

Compound fracture
Of the rump.

THE HUNTERS

My father is a sportsman
And a crack shot with his gun,
And when he lets me hunt with him
It's always lots of fun.

The outdoor part I quite enjoy,
But I can't seem to stifle
The feeling that each duck out there
Should also have a rifle.

I really like the animals;
I'm very tenderhearted,
And so I chase them all away
Before the hunt gets started.

The other guys are out there
Eating venison and duck,
While Dad and I have hot dogs
And complain about our luck.

So please don't tell him that his son
Is scaring off the game.
The deer and ducks and rabbits too
Will live to bless my name.

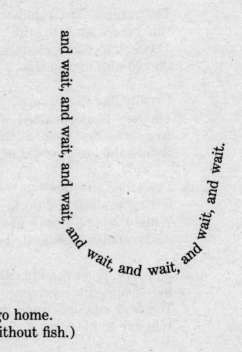

FISHING

Fishing —
I went once,
And I know everything about it.
Some people just can't live without it.
You bait your hook,

and wait, and wait, and wait, and wait, and wait, and wait, and wait, and wait.

Then you go home.
(Usually without fish.)

SUMO WRESTLING

You start with two guys wearing diapers of black,
Each one twice the size of a lummox.
They run at each other with earthshaking steps,
And pummel together their stomachs.

The *smack* is enormous, and all of that flesh
Just settles around them and jiggles.
All this is in silence, for nobody cheers.
(They're lucky that nobody giggles.)

You watch these two giants as they surge and they ram,
You see all that bulk in full flight.
You look at these athletes, and make up your mind —
You're starting that diet *tonight*!

THE GYMNASTICS TEAM

Kelly is awesome on uneven bars,
Brittany and Dawn are our two biggest stars.
Sandra's the queen of the floor exercise,
Dawn is real good at it too — big surprise.

Me? I have trouble just vaulting the horse.
All of the others can do it, of course.
Each time I fall like a rock from the beam,
They must all think, "How did *she* make this team?"

Well . . .

Even though all of the others are great,
Only *my* mom has a van that seats eight.
Not even Dawn can be light on her feet
If no one gives her a ride to the meet!

CAMPING AT
GLACIER RANGE

Camping is the life, my boy!
To live outdoors!
Be free!
There isn't any outlet here
to plug in the TV!

We'll swim out in the ice-cold lake!
We'll fish for what we eat!
A snake the size of Ogopogo
just attacked my feet!

We'll hike until the day's last light
is gone without a trace!
I wonder how the Cubs made out.
Oh, man, I hate this place!

When you're out in the wilderness,
you always sleep the best!
That tent hole's big enough
to land a spaceship on my chest!

And what a hearty appetite!
You eat until you burst!
I'm sure I'll really savor
what the insects don't get first!

It's such a pristine setting —
it's impossible to spoil it!
Bad news — a grizzly bear just
stole our only Porta-Toilet!

The quiet and the solitude —
it's something I hold dear!
I'd like to put an 80-story
building up right here!

It's time to put our gear away.
Tonight is our last night.
I couldn't get that lucky!
I'm hallucinating, right?

And so we bid a fond farewell
to lovely Glacier Range.
Good. Let some other sucker freeze
his butt off for a change!

EPILOGUE

On Jeremy's birthday, his parents presented him with a brand-new computer.

"We were thinking of getting you football pads," Mrs. Bloom explained. "But you've been doing so much writing lately that we decided you'd get a lot more use out of this."

Jeremy and his father carried the big boxes to his room, and unpacked the new machine.

"The wiring in this old house wasn't made for such advanced technology," Mr. Bloom warned. "So make sure nobody uses anything electric until I've got the computer all hooked up."

Jeremy watched as his father carefully attached the keyboard, the monitor, and the printer.

He was distracted by the doorbell: *ding do* ——

Before the *dong* ever finished, there was a *pop!* and a shower of sparks sprayed from the wall plug, and traveled up the cable to the computer.

"Ow!" Mr. Bloom dropped the mouse and jumped back.

BOOM! The monitor exploded, sending shattered glass all over Jeremy's desk and carpet. A plume of smoke hung like a black cloud over the corpse of the computer.

Jeremy ran to the front door and opened it. There on his front stoop stood Mrs. Stegowitz.

"Jeremy, I have wonderful news!" she gushed. "I've convinced the principal to change your grade to A plus for *both* years you were in my class!"

"That's great, Mrs. Stegowitz." Jeremy smiled sadly.

"You really are a talented poet," the teacher went on. "In fact, you should consider getting a computer for your writing."

"I had one," he replied, brushing the fresh ashes from his shirt, "for about thirty seconds. But somebody fried it."

Later, at Jeremy's birthday party, Michael and Chad listened in wide-eyed horror as Jeremy recounted the story.

"Man!" breathed Michael. "You must have wanted to kill her!"

"Nah!" laughed Jeremy. "She can ruin my career in sports, and blow up my computer, but not even Mrs. Stegosaurus can destroy a manufacturer's warranty!"

ABOUT THE AUTHORS

Bernice Korman and Gordon Korman make up one of the few mother-and-son poetry-writing teams in the world today. Their first collection, *The D–Poems of Jeremy Bloom*, was so popular that they decided to write a sequel. Gordon wrote his first book, *This Can't Be Happening at Macdonald Hall!*, for a seventh-grade English project. Bernice entered the business when Gordon conned her into typing it for him.

Bernice lives in Thornhill, Ontario, with her husband. Gordon lives with his wife in Florida and New York. He has written more than twenty books for middle-grade and young-adult readers, including seven books in the well-known Bruno and Boots series. His latest book is *The Chicken Doesn't Skate*, also published by Scholastic.